# Note to parents, carers and teachers

*Read it yourself* is a series of modern stories, favourite characters and traditional tales written in a simple way for children who are learning to read. The books can be read independently or as part of a guided reading session.

Each book is carefully structured to include many high-frequency words vital for first reading. The sentences on each page are supported closely by pictures to help with understanding, and to offer lively details to talk about.

The books are graded into four levels that progressively introduce wider vocabulary and longer stories as a reader's ability and confidence grows.

## Ideas for use

- Begin by looking through the book and talking about the pictures. Has your child heard this story before?

- Help your child with any words he does not know, either by helping him to sound them out or supplying them yourself.

- Developing readers can be concentrating so hard on the words that they sometimes don't fully grasp the meaning of what they're reading. Answering the puzzle questions on pages 30 and 31 will help with understanding.

*For more information and advice on Read it yourself and book banding, visit* **www.ladybird.com/readityourself**

Book Band 7

**Level 2** is ideal for children who have received some reading instruction and can read short, simple sentences with help.

## Special features:

Frequent repetition of main story words and phrases

Short, simple sentences

The king and queen fell asleep, and everybody in the castle fell asleep.

Years went by and thorns grew on the castle.

Large, clear type

The prince cut down the thorns and went in the castle.

He looked at the sleeping princess.

"How beautiful she is!" he said.

Careful match between story and pictures

Educational Consultant: Geraldine Taylor
Book Banding Consultant: Kate Ruttle

A catalogue record for this book is available from the British Library

Published by Ladybird Books Ltd
80 Strand, London, WC2R 0RL
A Penguin Company

001

© LADYBIRD BOOKS LTD MMX. This edition MMXIII
Ladybird, Read It Yourself and the Ladybird Logo are registered or
unregistered trademarks of Ladybird Books Limited.

ISBN: 978-0-72327-292-2

Printed in China

# Sleeping Beauty

Illustrated by Richard Johnson

A king and queen had a baby girl. The good fairies came to see her.

"How beautiful she is!" they said.

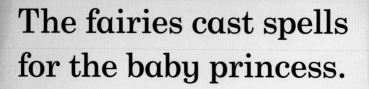

The fairies cast spells
for the baby princess.

"She will be kind,"
said one fairy.

"She will be clever,"
said another fairy.

9

Then, a bad fairy came in.
She looked at the
baby princess.

"How beautiful she is!"
said the bad fairy.

11

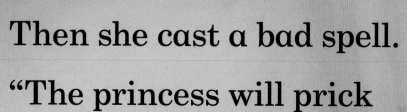

Then she cast a bad spell.

"The princess will prick
her finger and die!"
she said.

But then a good fairy
cast a spell.
"The princess will not die.
She will prick her finger
and fall asleep for
one hundred years."

Years went by and the princess grew more kind and more beautiful.

One day, the princess found a spinning wheel and pricked her finger.

She fell asleep.

The king and queen
fell asleep, and everybody
in the castle fell asleep.

Years went by and thorns
grew on the castle.

One hundred years
went by.

Then one day, a prince
came to the castle.

23

The prince cut down
the thorns and went
in the castle.

He looked at the
sleeping princess.

"How beautiful she is!"
he said.

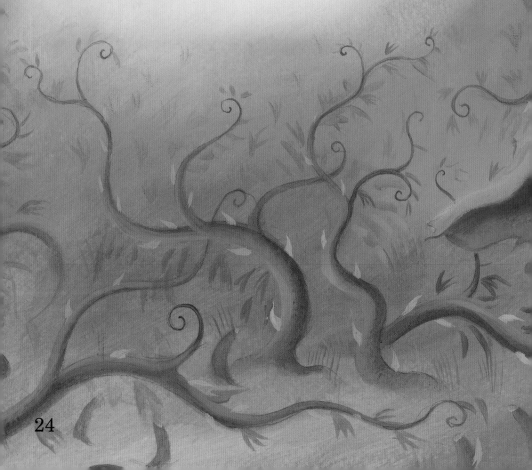

The prince gave the sleeping princess a kiss and she woke up.

The king and queen woke up, and everybody in the castle woke up, too.

"Will you marry me?"
said the prince.

"Yes," said the princess.
So she did!

How much do you remember about the story of Sleeping Beauty? Answer these questions and find out!

- What spell does the bad fairy cast?

- What does Sleeping Beauty prick her finger on?

- How long does everyone fall asleep for?

- How does the prince wake up Sleeping Beauty?

**Look at the pictures and match them to the story words.**

princess

spinning wheel

prince

castle

fairy

# Read it yourself with Ladybird

## Tick the books you've read!

For beginner readers who can read short, simple sentences with help.

**Level 2**

 Beauty and the Beast ☐

 Chicken Licken ☐

 Little Red Riding Hood ☐

 Nature Trail ☐

 Sports Day ☐

 Pirate School ☐

 Rumpelstiltskin ☐

 Sleeping Beauty ☐

 The Gingerbread Man ☐

 Sly Fox and Red Hen ☐

 The Tale of Jemima Puddle-Duck ☐

 The Three Little Pigs ☐

 Why Lion ROARRRS! ☐

 The Big Race ☐

 Town Mouse and Country Mouse ☐

 Dan's Dragon ☐

For more confident readers who can read simple stories with help.

**Level 3**

 You won't like this present as much as I do! ☐

 The Elves and the Shoemaker ☐

 Hansel and Gretel ☐

 Harry and the Bucketful of Dinosaurs ☐

 Jack and the Beanstalk ☐

 Furi on Music Island ☐

 Poppet Stows Away ☐

 Rapunzel ☐

 The Red Knight ☐

 Available on the App Store

The Read it yourself with Ladybird app is now available for iPad, iPhone and iPod touch

App also available on Android devices